The Angel in Red High Tops

The Angel in Red High Tops

By Anne Parker and Helen Cleveland
Illustrated by
Margaret Anne Suggs

Published by G. Angel Corps

Published by G. Angel Corps

Manufactured in the United States of America
Library of Congress Catalog Card Number: 96-084368
ISBN 0-939801-07-8

First printing, September 1996

The reproduction of the art for this book was accomplished using filmless, computer-driven cameras at
CMYK Digital, Atlanta, Ga. 30324

Acknowledgements:

We would like to express our deepest gratitude to Rex Hauck, "The Angel Man," for his inspiration and encouragement. Rex is an Emmy Award winning writer whose book *Angels, the Mysterious Messengers*, inspired the NBC Television movie series "Angels I" and "Angels II". Also, a special thanks to Duncan Dobie, author of *If You've Ever Seen A Rhinoceros Charge...* for his enthusiastic help and editorial assistance in producing this book.

This book is dedicated to the memory of my mother,
Kathryn Webster Barnett. "Told you so."

ABP

"Let's plan a crazy new adventure today," Jimmy said to his brother one Saturday morning. "I'm bored."

"Right," Mack replied. "A crazy new adventure... You know Mom doesn't like **your** new adventures. They're always dangerous."

"Mom always freaks at every little thing we do," Mack continued. "Even climbing that *little* old oak tree in the park gets her all upset."

"Yeah, you're right," Jimmy complained. "She even worries when we walk two blocks to the candy store. Too bad Gram can't be in charge. She *never* seems to worry about us."

"Right," Mack agreed. "She's **SO** cool. She *never* freaks out."

"Gram says she doesn't worry about us because that's our angels' job," Jimmy explained. "According to Gram, we all have our very own personal guardian angels."

"Right," repeated Mack. "We all have accordion angels."

"Not *accordion* angels!" Jimmy said with a wince. "*According* to her, we have *guardian* angels!"

"Right," Mack said, feeling a little mixed up and embarrassed. "We all have *guardian* angels."

"Gram says everybody has a guardian angel," Jimmy said. "Mothers, fathers, uncles, aunts — even grandparents."

"Even kids?" Mack asked.

"Especially kids!" Jimmy answered. "According to Gram, kids need them the most."

"Gram says angels have always been with us," Jimmy continued. "God gives one to everybody in the whole world. Gram believes angels are God's helpers and they watch over us every day of our lives forever and ever."

"If everybody's got one, then how come I've never seen mine?" Mack asked with a puzzled look.

"Gram says they're invisible," Jimmy answered.

"But if they're invisible, how would you know if you have one?" Mack asked.

"Maybe it's kind of like love," Jimmy said. "Love is invisible, too, but you feel it inside... in your **heart**."

"Maybe," said Mack. "but I'd still like to see mine."

"Maybe you will, someday," Jimmy said.

"Right," Mack said, sounding doubtful.

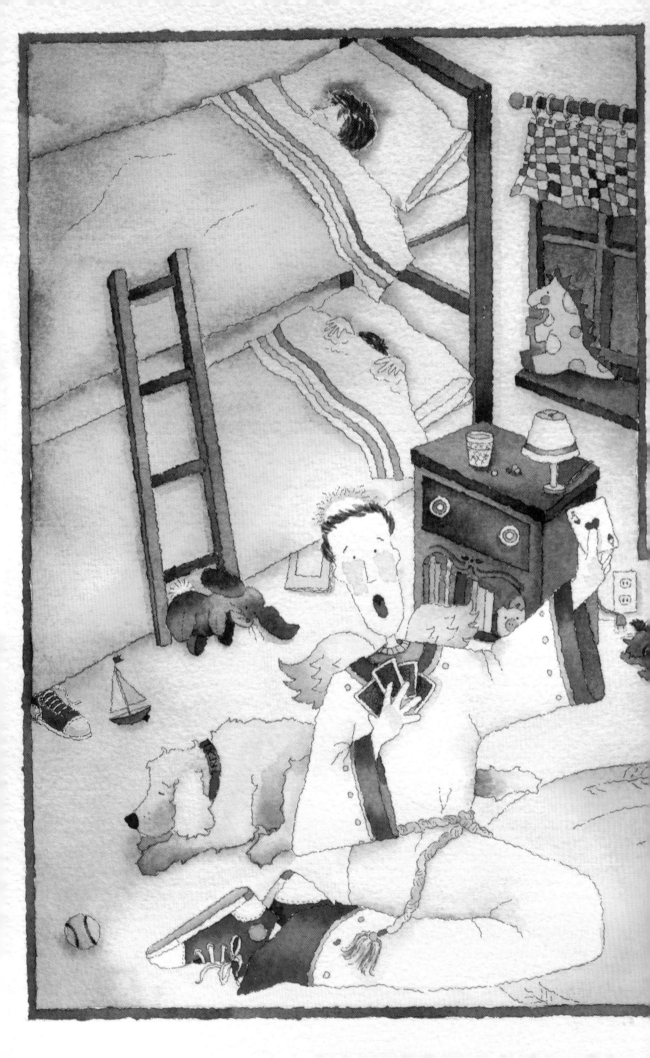

That night, Jimmy and Mack lay in bed, thinking about angels.

"Okay, if you really are here, guardian angel, make my back-yard into a **giant** baseball field," Jimmy whispered. He waited, but nothing happened.

"Well, then make a dinosaur appear in my window," Jimmy whispered again. Still, nothing happened.

Jimmy sighed and tried one more time. "Okay," he said. "Then do something easy. Make my light come on." Jimmy waited and waited, but the light never came on. Finally, he rolled over and went to sleep.

Mack was still awake. "If I really do have a guardian angel watching over me, then he must be the most bored angel in the whole world," Mack said to himself. "I never do anything daring. I'm always too scared to be brave." With that, he pulled the covers up over his eyes and drifted off to sleep.

The next morning, the two boys were out riding their bikes. Jimmy had his mind on other things, but Mack was still thinking about guardian angels.

Maybe only the **WILD** kids get angels, Mack thought. Maybe they're the only ones who really need them.

Then Jimmy called out. "Race you to the bottom of the hill!"

Mack had always been afraid to race, but today, even **he** felt a little brave.

As Mack reached for his helmet, Jimmy was already speeding toward the end of the block.

Mack gripped the handlebars tightly as he peddled down the hill. The wind felt good on his face.

Jimmy looked back at Mack. Suddenly, Jimmy's front tire hit a big rock, causing him to lose control and crash. His bike flipped over, throwing him to the ground.

Mack gasped as he crouched lower and sped to his brother's rescue. When he got closer to Jimmy, he was relieved to see that Jimmy's only injury was a scraped knee. Thankful that his brother was all right, Mack smiled the biggest smile ever!

All at once, Mack saw the approaching car. It was coming up the hill, and was headed straight for him.

"Oh, no!" Mack cried. "Please help me! Please, **someone**, help me!"

Mack closed his eyes and gripped the handlebars even tighter. The car was just about to hit him when a strange force seemed to lift him from the bike. He sailed through the air and tumbled softly onto the grass of a neighbor's front yard.

It took a second for Mack to catch his breath. Looking up, he saw the most incredible sight he had ever seen. It looked just like a man, but he knew it had to be **his angel!** The angel was dressed in a long white robe. He had a pair of small wings and a golden halo over his head. But the thing that amazed Mack most of all was what the angel had on *under* his robe. He was wearing a pair of bright red high tops, just like Mack's.

"Oh, my gosh! You really did come!" Mack stammered, barely able to whisper. "You came right when I needed you."

The angel nodded. "Actually, I've **always** been with you," he said in a friendly tone.

Mack was more confused than ever. He didn't understand. "If I've never seen you before, how could you always be with me?" he asked.

"Remember the time when you got lost in the park and a really nice old lady took you by the hand and brought you back to your mother?" the angel asked. "Well, that really nice old lady was me."

"In a disguise?" Mack asked.

"Angels come in m**a**ny different forms," the angel answered.

"I remember now!" Mack said excitedly. "You were wearing a purple coat and you had on red high tops then, too. Just like **I** wear!"

"That's right," the angel said. "You have a good memory, Mack. And how about the time your teacher, Mrs. Humphries, asked you to sing a solo in the Christmas pageant? You were so afraid that you didn't think you could do it. But when the night of the pageant arrived, you were **GREAT** ! Everyone said you sang just like an angel. Remember the standing ovation?"

"That was you?" Mack asked.

The angel nodded and puffed up with pride.

"And when I caught that long fly ball to win the game for my baseball team," Mack asked. "Was that you, too?"

The angel smiled warmly. "No, Mack, that was you. You did that entirely on your own. I was there watching, and you were GREAT !"

Mack felt very small and undeserving. "Don't you get bored watching out *just* for me?" he asked. "I mean, I'm not as brave as my brother. I don't see how **I** could ever do enough to keep you busy."

The angel laughed. "Mack, getting bored is something that **never** happens to angels. You're very special to me, and I like watching out for you. Sure, you're different from Jimmy, but you're a lot braver than you think. You can call me A^NY time. Angels like to stay busy!"

"Do you have a phone?" Mack asked.

"No," the angel answered with a big grin. "Guardian angels don't need phones, Mack. Just listen to your **heart** and think of me, and you'll never be alone. I'm **always** with you!"

Several of Mack's neighbors had gathered around to see if he was all right. The driver of the car had gotten out, and Jimmy was standing close by. Even Gram had rushed outside after hearing the screeching of the tires.

"It was like **magic**!" a child in the crowd said loudly. "Mack looked like he was *floating* through the air."

"Was it magic?" Mack asked, looking up at his angel.

"No, Mack, it wasn't magic," the angel answered. "What happened here today was very real. And now that I know you're okay, I'd better be going. It's time for me to check in with the boss. It seems like I'm always on the run. That's why I like to wear red high tops."

"But will I ever see you again?" Mack asked.

"Maybe," said the angel. "But even if you can't see me, remember that I am **always** with you."

The angel reached down and touched Mack's **heart** as only angels can do. Mack felt a special *tingling* deep inside. Then the angel disappeared.

Suddenly, Mack realized that Jimmy and Gram were standing next to him. Gram smiled affectionately. She looked up, then in a low tone that only the two boys could hear, she whispered, "Told you so."

Dear Kids -

If you would like to share YOUR
angel story, please write to us!
We would L♥VE to hear from you.

Angel Stories
P.O. Box 550726
Atlanta, GA 30305

Anne & Helen

About the Authors:

Anne Barnett Parker (left) was born in New Orleans. She graduated from the University of Virginia. After college, Anne moved to Atlanta, where she currently resides with her husband, John, and their three children, Blair, Britton, and John. Not long ago, Anne's angel convinced her to consider writing a children's book about guardian angels that could help teach children about the important roles angels play in their lives. A short time later, she persuaded her friend Helen to join her on this adventure. With much guidance from their angels, *The Angel in Red High Tops* was created.

Helen Jarvis Cleveland (right) grew up in New Jersey. She came South to attend the University of Georgia. For many years she has lived in Atlanta with her husband, "Coach" Dave, and their three very active sons, Gamble, Kent, and Mac. Helen's house is always filled with animals, neighborhood kids, and lots of busy angels. Each of her boys has a special relationship with an angel, and all of the angels in the Cleveland household have been personally named!

About the Illustrator:

Shortly after Helen Cleveland and Anne Parker teamed up to write this book, Anne's angel was very instrumental in tracking down Georgia artist Margaret Anne Suggs. Margaret was born in Mobile, Alabama, and grew up in Atlanta. She received her BFA from Auburn University. Margaret is now pursuing her masters degree in art in Dublin, Ireland. Her own guardian angel, who happens to wear espadrilles, has always been very close to her heart. For this reason, Margaret was very excited about illustrating *The Angel in Red High Tops*!